Do you ever feel sad?

Everyone feels sad sometimes, even people who don't seem that way on the outside.

Little Miss Giggles felt sad when she lost her giggle.

And Mr Tickle felt sad when there was no one to tickle.

Until he met Little Miss Giggles and both of them were happy after a tickle or two!

MR. MEN
LITTLE MISS
Feeling Sad

Roger Hargreaves

Original concept by
Roger Hargreaves

With grateful thanks to

700045972935

This is a story about feeling sad.

There are many different reasons why you might feel sad.

Mr Jelly is frightened of everything. Even a leaf falling from a tree can make him quiver and tremble and turn to jelly.

Being scared of things can make him feel like he's missing out. And feeling this way, makes him sad.

One day, Mr Jelly was feeling particularly sad.

That morning a cheeping bird had startled him and he'd spilt all his breakfast.

Then Mr Jelly had been too nervous to go and buy some more milk in case there was a huge flock of gulls outside his house.

Of course, there wasn't!

Fortunately, Little Miss Curious had noticed that Mr Jelly was feeling sad and she was curious to see if there was anything that would help him to feel happier.

Do you try to cheer up your friends when they're feeling sad?

Little Miss Curious decided to invite Mr Jelly to Nonsenseland!

"I hear it's a really fun and silly place and I'd love you to join me on a daytrip," she said. "Hopefully it will brighten your day too!"

Little Miss Curious had never been to Nonsenseland, so she was excited to explore.

Unfortunately, Mr Jelly was less than excited.

In fact, his heart sank at the thought of going somewhere so unfamiliar.

"Thanks for inviting me, Little Miss Curious," he said timidly, "but I think I'll just stay here. My day isn't going very well so far and anything could happen to me in Nonsenseland."

"Don't worry, Mr Jelly," replied Little Miss Curious, reassuringly. "I'll be with you and we'll face these new experiences together."

How do you feel about going somewhere new?

After some gentle persuasion, Mr Jelly agreed to visit Nonsenseland as long as they could leave if he was really unhappy.

Have you ever heard of Nonsenseland?

Maybe you've read a story or two that took place there.

Well, Little Miss Curious was in for a surprise as it is like nowhere else!

In Nonsenseland, everything is as silly as can be.

The trees are pink and the grass is blue.

In Nonsenseland, dogs wear hats and birds fly backwards.

Isn't that silly?

When they arrived, Mr Jelly was very quiet, trying to take it all in. While Little Miss Curious was full of questions.

"Why is your house in a tree?" she asked Mr Nonsense.

"So I'm closer to the ground," he replied with a confident smile.

As you may have realised, Mr Nonsense makes no sense at all!

Mr Jelly was beginning to get used to Nonsenseland. It wasn't the scary place he'd imagined.

But Little Miss Curious really wanted to understand why things in Nonsenseland are so different, so she tried asking Mr Silly some questions.

"Why does that car have square wheels?" she asked.

"So it doesn't roll down the hill," he replied.

I'm sure you won't be surprised to hear that gave Little Miss Curious even more questions.

But as you may have noticed, Mr Jelly is smiling.

"That's very funny, Mr Silly," chuckled Mr Jelly.

"Meow," agreed a chicken, walking by in his wellington boots, carrying an umbrella.

Nonsenseland animals don't make the same noises as those where you live!

Mr Jelly's smile turned into a chuckle and his body shook happily because he was laughing so much.

"Thank you, Little Miss Curious," he laughed. "I don't feel sad anymore being surrounded by all these marvellously silly things!"

Have you ever found that a bit of silliness helps to lift your mood?

Sadly Little Miss Curious didn't feel the same. She had a sinking feeling in her tummy.

Being somewhere completely silly had brightened Mr Jelly's mood and lifted his sadness, but it had actually made Little Miss Curious feel a little downhearted and confused.

"That's really good news, Mr Jelly," she said quietly. "Would you mind if we left now?"

"But there's much more to see," he replied with a puzzled expression. "Aren't you curious about what you might be missing out on?"

Little Miss Curious decided to be brave and tell Mr Jelly how she was feeling.

"Being somewhere new and different isn't what I expected it to be like," she said sadly. "I'm finding it hard and feeling a bit sad. What should I do?"

"Oh, Little Miss Curious. It's OK to feel sad sometimes," he replied, thoughtfully. "It can be hard when we have emotions that don't feel good, but those feelings are just a small part of who you are."

What do you do when you're feeling sad?

Little Miss Curious found it helped talking to Mr Jelly, who was very understanding.

"You can't be happy all the time," he said wisely. "It's OK to be sad sometimes. In fact it can help us learn a lot about our own feelings and those of other people."

"Thank you, Mr Jelly. I love nothing better than learning about things," Little Miss Curious smiled.

In helping Mr Jelly, Little Miss Curious had learnt a bit more about herself too.

They were also both about to learn something surprising about Nonsenseland snow.

Without any warning, a huge flurry of yellow snowdrops fell from the sky and a thick layer settled on the ground!

Yes, yellow snow! In Nonsenseland the snow is as yellow as custard.

Little Miss Curious had one more question …

"Do you want a snowball fight?"

And a barrage of yellow snowballs came back as the happy reply!